To Eva and Milton

CALLAWAY

64 Bedford Street
New York, New York 10014

When I Have a Little Girl/When I Have a Little Boy. Revised text copyright © 2000 by Charlotte Zolotow
When I Have a Little Girl/When I Have a Little Boy. Revised pictures copyright © 2000 by Hilary Knight

When I Have a Little Girl was originally published in 1965. It was published in slightly different form than this edition.

Printed in China by Palace Press International

First Edition
10 9 8 7 6 5 4 3 2 1
Library of Congress Cataloging-in-Publication Data available.
ISBN 0-935112-45-6

Visit Callaway at www.callaway.com

Antoinette White, Senior Editor • True Sims, Director of Production • Toshiya Masuda, Designer

When I Have a Little Girl

by Charlotte Zolotow

pictures by Hilary Knight

CALLAWAY NEW YORK

2000

W hen I have a little girl . . .

She can wear party dresses to school.

She can be fresh to unpleasant people.

She can go through all my bureau drawers . . .

and try on rings and bracelets and scarves without asking.

She can have a party every week . . .

and go to a restaurant once a month
and order whatever she wants.

She can go without a coat or hat or boots . . .

the very first warm day . . .

even if it snows again later.

Ｓhe can let her hair grow . . . . as long as she wants.

And one bath a week will be enough.

And nobody will tell her in winter to stop eating snow.

Or in summer to come out of the ocean even if she is turning blue.

She can touch the fur collars of ladies in front of her

on the bus or train . . .

or standing in line.

And she can pat any dog she wants
without asking if it's friendly.
(She'll know. I always do.)

She can tell anything she wants about
me to anyone she wants.

She can always answer the phone and talk first
to anyone who calls even if it's business.

She can have a new box of crayons every week even if
the older ones are still good and just not pointed anymore.

She can uncover the leaves around the crocus shoots and
then cover them up if it should snow again.

She won't have to be home before dark,
so she will be able to see the moon rise.

And she can get up in the morning before it's light and go out in her nightgown to watch the sun come up.

She can give milk to all the cats
and if they don't go away afterward . . .

they can live with her.

When I have a little girl
all the rules will be different.

And I will never say to her,
"When you are a mother you will
understand why all these rules
are necessary."

My mother says . . .

her mother used to say it too.

This is a flip-flop book, so please flip-flop it over to see what will happen when I have a little boy.

he was late for his lesson.

This is a flip-flop book, so please flip-flop it over to see what will happen when I have a little girl.

and he'll never have to take piano.

and John had to run because

He can run around

and up and down

and around

and around

and shout as loudly as he wants

He can have a pet monkey and climb the bookcase and take apart alarm clocks

and play the radio and TV full volume so it sounds good.

He can have triple malteds just before dinner

and plain mustard sandwiches on rye.

He can come to all the grownup parties.

He'll never have to go to sleep till he finishes the chapter   and he can do his homework at the last minute.

He can talk while we're fishing, my son.

He can stay down at the railroad station all day

watching trains come and counting the freight cars.

He won't have to talk to any girls, especially his mother's friend's daughter.

He'll never have to play with his father's friend's son or say thank you for presents he hates.

He can go out without saying goodbye

and come home without saying hello.
He'll have a key of his own.

He can sleep in the yard on hot summer nights

and see the movie over and over until the theater closes.

Or wear earmuffs in winter, even if his ears turn red.

He can wear jeans all the time, even to birthday parties, and no socks.

He will never have to have his hair cut, my son.

he won't have to take piano

or have shots

Michael and John were walking home from school. They couldn't play because John had a piano lesson.

When I have a son, John said,

When I Have a Little Boy

by Charlotte Zolotow

PICTURES by Hilary Knight

CALLAWAY  NEW YORK

2000

For a wonderful teacher, Helen C. White

CALLAWAY

64 Bedford Street
New York, New York 10014

Printed in China by Palace Press International
First Edition
10 9 8 7 6 5 4 3 2 1

Library of Congress Cataloging-in-Publication Data available.
ISBN 0-935112-45-6

Visit Callaway at www.callaway.com

Antoinette White, Senior Editor • True Sims, Director of Production • Toshiya Masuda, Designer